The Most Wonderful Game

Liam Ford

ISBN 978-0-9959075-8-4

To M.C.

for playing the game with me

• • •

ABRAHAM WAS ALONE playing with his toys.

The knight on the white horse with black markings rode towards the immense grey castle.

"State your name," the guard called from the parapet, "and what business you have at Rivertide."

"I have come," the knight yelled through his helmet, "at the bidding of good King Garderik."

"And you are?"

"Sir Calidas."

The drawbridge dropped with a thud and the massive wooden doors swung open. The knight pulled on the reins. The horse reared with a fearsome whinny and galloped across and through.

"My lord," the knight said, kneeling and removing his helmet to hold in the crook of his arm.

“Rise, rise!” the king declared, lifting his arms. “Sir Calidas, it is I who should be kneeling to you!” The knight remained on his knee. “A true gentleman you are.”

“My liege.” He bowed deeper.

“Enough with the pleasantries. You know why I have summoned you — and you alone?”

The knight knew but kept his mouth shut.

“Truly you are the most gallant knight in the realm. And valiant! You shall need all of your noble qualities to achieve the quest—”

“Abraham!” Mom called from upstairs. “Dinner time!”

He sighed and dropped the knight. Coming, he thought.

Mom and Dad were sitting at the table. Abraham sat and served himself. Lasagna, Caesar salad, garlic bread.

“So I told Johnson that if it was a yes-man he was looking for, he’d have to look somewhere else.” Dad forked pasta into his mouth, oil glistening on his well-trimmed moustache. Sauce spattered his white dress shirt undone at the collar.

“Oh dear,” Mom said, squinting, “don’t tell me—”

Dad’s fork drooped. “Don’t ‘oh dear’ me!”

Mom held his gaze. “You lost your job, didn’t you.”

“I didn’t lose it.” His fork hit the plate. “It’s not like it disappeared. ‘Oh, where did my job go?’” He looked around the dining room at the paisley papered walls, the mirrored cabinet filled with glistening crystal figurines. “‘Have you seen my job? I don’t know where it went!’”

Mom rolled her eyes.

"I didn't lose my job, dear, I quit!" The legs squealed as he pushed his chair back and stomped out.

Eyes stinging, Abraham looked at Mom.

She half-smiled. "So, how was your day, honey?"

After dinner Abraham cleared the table, rinsed the dishes and put them in the dishwasher. He did his homework and watched a half-hour of TV with the volume down low so it didn't bug Dad, who was reading a detective novel in the recliner behind him.

"Time for bed, honey," Mom said.

He changed into pyjamas, brushed his teeth and got under the sheets. Mom poked her head in. "Good night, honey." She switched off the light and closed the door.

"Good night," Abraham said.

They were the first words he'd spoken all day.

One

"GOOD MORNING, CLASS!"

"Good morning, Mrs. Picadia," the class intoned.

Abraham mouthed the words. He doubted Mrs. P noticed, with her thick, cat-eye glasses and the frizzy dyed-black perm muffling her ears.

"We have a new student joining us today, and I'd like you all to welcome her to the class. Welcome, Mya!"

She was short with long, straight black hair, brown skin — like the walls of the rumpus room, Abraham thought — and brown eyes that shone as bright as Mom's crystal knick-knacks.

"Welcome, Mya," the class said.

She smiled and looked at each student in turn. "Thank you, Mrs. P, and thank you, fellow students. I'm excited to learn and play with all of you!"

"Aren't you quite the charming little girl! Now let's see if your reading is as strong as your public speaking. Can you please open your textbook and start reading at 'There is an old story...'"

*

Abraham watched the kids chase the ball up and down the field, yelling and laughing under the blue sky and white clouds. He looked down at the gravel and dragged his toe sideways. He turned back towards the school. The bell would ring any minute.

The new girl was standing near the door to the classroom. "Hello!" she said, fixing him with her dazzling eyes. "What's your name?"

He knew his name, but—

"Shy, are you? That's okay. My name's Mya. How come you aren't playing soccer with the other kids?"

Nobody asked me to play, he thought.

"It's kind of a silly game, isn't it? Running back and forth like a crazy person chasing a ball. And only being allowed to touch it with your feet? My dad and brother are crazy about it. They watch it on TV and yell at the screen as if the players could hear them." She giggled. It sounded like it was coming from somewhere else. "Sorry I'm talking so much. I'm nervous, I guess." She scrunched up her eyes and peered into Abraham's. "Well, I hope we can be friends. I don't have any friends here, and all my dad and brother like to do is watch TV and play soccer. He's a coach, you know. If you ever want to—"

The bell rang and the door to the classroom opened. Abraham scurried inside to his desk.

After school Abraham saw the new girl standing at the fence on the edge of the grounds looking back towards the building.

When she left Abraham walked home behind her. She turned into the yard in front of a small, one-storey brown house. He watched her walk up to the door, look behind her and go in.

Two

THE HORSE'S HOOVES thundered along the rocky trail. Sir Calidas rode hard, driving Cygnus into the dark wood. There was no time to waste.

Princess Devada — the king's only daughter and the heiress to the throne — had wandered off alone, lured by the full moon and a spell cast by the meddling druid mage Okenower (or so the king suspected). Whatever the reason, Calidas's task was to retrieve the maiden before any danger befell her.

He dug in his spurs. Cygnus was frothing already but a rubdown and fresh straw awaited him at the royal stables were he — were they — successful. And if they weren't... Calidas shuddered. The king's wrath was as extreme as his kindness. And Calidas knew which he'd rather incur.

The knight looked skyward. A wisp of dark cloud snaked across the cratered moon. A howl sounded from the darkness ahead. The tree branches sprang back ahead of him and snapped shut behind.

"Faster, Cygnus, faster!"

"Abraham!" It was Mom. He dropped the toy.

*

"Now class… Who can tell me which country has the largest population in the world?"

Abraham raised his hand. A few other hands went up, arms bent at the elbows, fingers trembling.

"Yes Ryan."

"China!"

"Very good, Ryan! Yes, it's China. Also the fourth biggest country by size." Mrs. P licked her finger and swiped the page. "Now. Who can tell me the country with the second" — Abraham raised his hand — "largest population?"

Ryan shrank in his seat. Somebody else's hand crept upward.

"Sarah?"

"Pakistan?"

"No, it's not Pakistan. But very, very close! Any other guesses?"

Abraham's hand was still up.

"Mya? Do you know the answer?"

She looked at Abraham then back to the teacher. "I think Abraham does."

"Yes, but I'm asking you."

"Russia? I think." She smiled.

"Oh, Mya! That's so close too!" Mrs. P adjusted her glasses. "But the answer is" — she looked at the textbook — "India."

Abraham let his hand fall. Mya looked at him and shrugged.

*

At recess, Abraham watched the kids standing on either side of a pole waiting for the ball and the rope tied to the top to wrap all the way around.

"What's that game?"

It was the new girl. "Tetherball."

"Tetherball? That's a funny name. Why's it called that?" Her dazzling eyes stared into his.

"Tethered means tied. The rope's tied to the pole, and the ball's tied to the rope."

"Makes sense." The ball hit the pole and bounced back. "You knew the answer to that question, didn't you?"

"India and Pakistan were the same country until 1947. The biggest population group is the Hindus. They have three principal gods."

"Why didn't Mrs. P ask you?"

Abraham shrugged. The bell was going to ring soon. He started walking towards the classroom and Mya followed.

*

After school, Abraham saw Mya waiting by the fence. He cinched up his backpack and walked over.

She stopped when they got to her front yard. “Want to come in and play? I know the most wonderful game.”

“I have to go home right after school or my mom gets worried.”

“Okay.” Her smile fell. “Maybe we can play another day?”

*

Dad wasn’t wearing a dress shirt and he hadn’t shaved. Mom heaped a spoon of steaming beef and broccoli on his plate.

“So?” Dad said, licking his lips, “what’d you learn at school today?” He chewed with his mouth open and took a swig from a can of beer, dripping some down his bristly chin.

Abraham pushed a spear of broccoli around his plate with the tines of his fork.

“Well?” Dad pointed his cutlery at opposite walls.

Abraham hadn’t learned anything. He already knew everything Mrs. P had read out of the textbook. School bored him and talking about it bored him more.

“Nothing?” Dad looked at Mom and shook his head. A morsel of half-chewed meat fell out of his mouth.

"Dear," Mom said.

Dad dropped his cutlery and picked up the beer can. "Well let me tell you how my day was. I spent the morning circling ads in the paper. Then I drove around town pretending to be interested in jobs I'd rather hang myself than work at—"

"Dear!"

"And when the managers said they thought I was overqualified or too old or not the right fit, whatever that means, I had to say thanks for your time, I sure do appreciate it, I hope you'll consider me if something else comes up." He took a long drink. "Then I went to the next place and endured the same humiliation, only to come home to overcooked broccoli, cheap meat and a kid who won't even talk to me."

Mom glared at him. "Maybe I wouldn't have to cook cheap meat if—"

"Okay, okay. I'm sorry about that, hon. But Abraham, pay attention. Because your unemployable, over-the-hill old man is going to tell you the truth. Stay in school as long as you can. Get a good education and get to know your fellow students and yourself. Because once you're out in the real world, everybody's going to want to see that piece of paper and everybody's going to try to give you the run around. And if you don't tell them what's what and stand up for yourself, they're going to walk all over you." Dad picked up his fork, stabbed a strip of limp meat and slid it into his mouth.

Mom looked at the ceiling, blinking.

Abraham listened to the ticking of the clock.

*

"Can you come inside and play today? It really is the most wonderful game." Mya looked at Abraham with her gleaming black eyes.

He thought of the knight on horseback, the princess caught in the clutches of the evil wizard. "Okay, but I have to be home for dinner."

"Oh yay!" She smiled and opened the front door. "Oh, come in, please. This is so exciting. I've never played this game with anyone before."

Abraham took off his backpack and shoes. The house smelled funny, like spicy dust.

"My brother's at soccer practice and my dad's the coach, so they won't be home for a while."

"What about your mom?"

"Oh, she's dead. Come on, let me show you the playroom."

Mya led Abraham down the hallway. The wooden floor creaked underneath and the white walls were faded yellow. A cobweb hung in the corner.

She opened a door with a sparkly rainbow push-pinned to it.

The window was covered with a purple sheet. In the middle of the room Abraham saw a dollhouse taller than him. He stepped inside and Mya closed the door.

She reached into the dollhouse and pulled a string. A bulb illuminated, lighting the house from the inside and projecting silhouettes onto the bare walls.

She wants me to play with dolls? Abraham thought.

Mya pulled another string. The dollhouse began to rotate, and the shadows shrank and grew as they moved along the walls.

Abraham leaned closer. One of the dolls had glasses and short black hair cut in a bowl. Another doll had long, wavy red hair. Another one had cat-eye glasses. They looked familiar. "Did you make these?"

"Well, my mom made the dolls. I made the outfits."

"They're amazing!"

The shadows walked across the walls, growing, shrinking, growing, shrinking.

"So," Mya said, eyes dazzling, "are you ready to play the most wonderful game?"

*

It was dark out when Abraham left.

"Oh thank god," Mom said when he walked in the door. She was sitting beside Dad on the couch, the cordless phone on the coffee table in front of them.

"Your mom — we — were worried sick," Dad said. "When you didn't come home for dinner, well." He cleared his throat. "Come here."

Mom and Dad crouched. Abraham walked over and they wrapped their arms around him.

"You must be hungry," Mom said, wiping her cheeks. "How would you like to have ice cream for dinner?"

?

THE SHADOWS ON THE WALLS grew and shrank, grew and shrank. One stopped moving, turned and swung its arms and legs. It was walking! The other shadows started doing the same. Abraham watched, fascinated, as they marched down the wall and stood in a circle around him, looking up.

Then he heard scissors opening and closing.

"Isn't this fun?" Mya said, scissors in hand. Her eyes were blazing like fire.

He tried to speak but couldn't. She held his wrist and put the blades around the first knuckle of his pinky finger. She closed the scissors. His fingertip separated like cut paper and floated to the ground. It didn't hurt. One of the shadows grabbed it and crammed it into its mouth.

He couldn't move so he watched as Mya cut his body into millions of little pieces and the shadows ate every single one.

Three

ABRAHAM WOKE UP and looked at his alarm clock. It was after 9.

He bolted upright. He was late! Why didn't Mom wake him up?

In the kitchen, Dad was frying bacon. Abraham rubbed his eyes. Dad only made breakfast on special occasions.

"There he is!" Dad said, looking over his shoulder. The bacon hissed and popped. "Have a good sleep?"

"Where's Mom?"

"She's reading the paper in bed. I figured I'd make breakfast, give her the day off, you know?" He dodged spitting grease. "Yow! Grab the pot and warm up her coffee, would ya?"

The bedroom door was open and Mom was propped up on the pillows.

"Hi honey! Came to offer me a refill, did you? Here." She put the newspaper down and held out her cup.

"How come you didn't wake me up this morning?"

"That's perfect, thanks. Well I figured you'd be exhausted after your adventure last night, so I called the school to let them know you wouldn't be coming in today."

"Really? But I'm fine... I can—"

"Nonsense. Here, I pulled out the comics. Get in and we can stay cozy until breakfast is ready."

After breakfast Mom cleared the dishes. "Looks like a beautiful day out there. Why don't you two run outside and play?"

Abraham looked at Dad. He could hardly remember the last time they played together. Would he even remember how?

"Sounds good to me." Dad leaned towards Abraham. "If I remember right, Sir Calidas was galloping into the dark forest on his trusty steed Cygnus. Get dressed and we'll see if we can find that sneaky evil-doer Okenower!"

Abraham got dressed.

Dad was waiting outside. "Ready?" He squatted and patted his back. "Hop on!"

Abraham threw his arms around Dad's neck. Dad stood and wrapped his arms around Abraham's legs. He whinnied like a horse and started running.

"Faster, Cygnus, faster!" Abraham yelled, laughing.

*

Cygnus slowed to a canter and sniffed at the ground.

"What is it, boy?" Calidas asked.

Cygnus snorted and shook his black-maned head.

“Wolves. I was afraid of that. It means Okenower can’t be far away.” Calidas snapped the reins and scanned the dark for movement. Cygnus froze — and reared. Calidas held on and reached for his scabbard. He raised his sword into the sky as a pack of mangy grey direwolves burst, snarling, from the trees and surrounded them.

“The hero has arrived,” a high-pitched voice sneered from the darkness. “But has he arrived in time?”

The wolves snapped their teeth. Circling, Cygnus kicked his back feet to ward them off.

“Show yourself, Okenower!” Calidas shouted. “Or are you as cowardly as your brother was?”

A flame appeared in the mouth of a cave, illuminating Okenower’s bearded, wizened face. He hissed, revealing the spaces where teeth used to be.

The wolves closed in. Cygnus loosed a terrified whinny.

“Is Princess Devada safe?” Calidas demanded.

The flame disappeared and reappeared. Firelight reflected off long, auburn tresses. “She is safe, but you and your horse” — in the blink of an eye Okenower was astride the largest of the wolves — “are in more danger than you could have imagined!”

The beast stood on its hind legs, slather dripping from its jagged maw. It howled.

Calidas tightened the reins. Cygnus stood, too, and towered over the mangy cur. His hooves struck the ground like a blacksmith’s hammer and they charged.

*

"Where have you boys been? I was about to send out the search party!" A pie was sitting on the counter and Mom was pulling a bubbling casserole from the oven. Shells and dogs! Abraham salivated.

Dad picked a twig from his sweater. "Oh, just saving Princess Devada from the clutches of an evil wizard, that's all."

"Well wash up, gallant knights, dinner's ready."

In between bites of gooey, chewy macaroni and cheese with slices of frankfurter, Abraham told Mom about their day.

"So it was all a clever ploy by Okenower to lure Sir Calidas to the woods so he could avenge his brother's death?" she asked.

"Yeah, but I figured that out ahead of time."

"And you went anyway?"

"Well, that's what a knight does, right?"

"A knight," Dad said, wiping cheese from his chin, "and his trusty steed."

Mom rolled her eyes.

"Of course," Abraham said. "He couldn't — I mean, I couldn't have done it without you."

"Who wants seconds?" Mom asked. Abraham and Dad raised their hands. She laughed. "Don't forget to save room for dessert!"

Dad washed the dishes, and Mom dried them and handed them to Abraham.

"Beside the fridge, bottom cupboard, to the left of the baking sheets, and ... go!"

Abraham took the cooling rack, spun around the island, dashed towards the fridge, crouched, opened the cupboard, slid the rack in, closed it and sprinted back.

"Three point two seconds!" Dad said. "New world record!" He pulled the sprayer from beside the faucet and blasted Abraham.

"Dear!" Mom said.

He turned the sprayer at her and squeezed. She squealed. Abraham laughed.

"Tell me when," Mom said, scooping ice cream from the pail. She dropped a scoop on his slice of pie and it started to melt. She scooped another. And another. She looked at Abraham.

"One more," he said, grinning.

Later, the crumb and cream-covered plates rested on the TV stands. The family leaned back on the couch, bellies bulging, laughing along with the television.

"Oh my god," Mom said, looking at the clock. "It's nearly 11!"

"So?" Dad said, smirking.

Mom smiled and shook her head. "Alright, one more show. But then it's bedtime — for all of us!"

Four

THE CHIRPING OF BIRDS woke Abraham.

A slant of sunlight glanced through the blinds. He watched the dust motes dance in the shafts of light.

There was a knock at the door.

Dad opened it and poked his head in. "Good morrow to thee, Sir Calidas. I'm off to a job interview. It's part-time and it pays really well, so I'll still have lots of time for adventures. Wish me luck!"

"Good luck, Cygnus! I mean, Dad!"

He whinnied and closed the door.

Abraham dozed off. When he woke up, Mom was hovering over him. "I'm meeting the ladies for coffee. Breakfast is on the table, and your lunch is in the fridge. Oh, and I called the school to have the bus pick you up so you don't have to walk." She kissed his forehead. "It will be here at 8:15. Have a great day, honey!"

*

The bus squealed to a stop at the top of the driveway and opened its door. Abraham cinched the straps of his backpack and got on.

"Well, good morning, Mr. Abraham!" said Mr. Hallick, the driver. "Glad you could join us today. Grab a seat and hold on!" The bus was full of laughing, jostling kids.

He walked down the aisle.

"Hi, Abraham!"

"Hey pal!"

"Abraham, what's up!"

"Abraham!" It was Sarah. "Come sit with me!"

His heart skipped a beat. He sat down. The smell of clean laundry wafted over him.

"I didn't know you lived around here?" She pulled her long, red hair behind her ears.

"Yeah... my whole life!"

She laughed. "That's so funny. Me too! How come I haven't seen you on the bus before?"

"Well, I ... It's my first time. I usually walk to school."

"Even in the rain?"

"Yup, even in the rain."

Her eyes widened. "Even in the snow?"

"Yup! Even in the snow!"

"Wow, that's so brave."

As they were piling off the bus, the bell rang. Abraham ran with the other kids towards the classroom. He and

Sarah got to the door at the same time. Her cheeks were red from running.

"After you," he said, sweeping his arm.

"What a gentleman!" she said, her cheeks turning redder.

"Good morning, class," Mrs. P said.

"Good morning, Mrs. Picadia."

Mya's desk was empty.

"I want to start today by returning your reports on the world's biggest countries. But before I do, I want to ask one student in particular to read out a section of theirs for all of us." She picked up a report from the top of the pile on her desk. Whispers filled the room. "Can you please come to the front of the class, Abraham?"

His chest warmed as the students turned to look at him. He cleared his throat and stood up. Heads turned as he walked to Mrs. P's desk.

Mrs. P leaned close and handed him his report. "This really is a fantastic report," she whispered. "You should be very proud."

On the cover was a big red A with three pluses beside it.

"Now, Abraham, if you'd like to read us the section you wrote on culture. Pay attention, class. I think you'll learn a lot."

Abraham opened the report. "'Hindus believe that the world was created by an all-knowing, all powerful god..."

At recess, Abraham stood on the edge of the field and watched the other kids run towards the centre. He looked around then down at the gravel.

"Hey Abraham!" It was Vince. He was holding the soccer ball in the crook of his arm, his blond hair almost white in the sunlight. "You wanna play?"

Abraham ran over and stood in a group with the other kids. Ryan nudged him with his elbow, nodded and pushed his glasses back up his nose.

"Okay," Vince said, drowning out the jokes and laughter. "I'm second captain, first pick."

"First captain, second pick," said a kid from another class.

Abraham looked down at his feet.

"Abraham," Vince said. He looked up. Vince waved him over. He looked at Ryan, who shrugged. The kids moved out of the way and he ran over. Vince handed him the ball.

After Ryan was picked, the teams took the field.

"Suzie and Tim," Vince said, "defence. Moe, goalie. Tracy, Tara, Colin — midfield. Jen? You're up front with me. Abraham, you too."

They took their positions. When the other team was ready, Abraham passed the ball across to Vince. He dribbled upfield, his check giving him lots of space. Abraham followed Vince's lead, staying in his lane up the left side. He glanced at his check, a tall skinny kid. Vince tapped the ball forward and broke into a run, catching his check off-guard. Abraham's check wasn't watching either so he ran around him into the clear.

As if Vince knew Abraham was open, he crossed the ball. Abraham caught it on the run and dribbled towards the net. A defender lunged to check Abraham but he lifted the ball over her foot and kept going. Glancing to his right, he saw Vince breaking towards the goal. He passed. Vince leapt. The ball connected with his foot and the keeper dove under it. The ball rippled the netting.

Vince threw his arms out and ran towards Abraham. "What a pass!"

"What a goal!" Abraham said, patting Vince's back.

"Nice one guys!"

"Way to go!"

Their opponents didn't let the early setback discourage them. They came on quick, overwhelming the defence, and tallied a fast evener. Abraham and Vince found their checks giving them less leeway so they depended on the midfielders to take off the pressure. When the defenders bit, Abraham and Vince found a gap. Vince took the pass and quickly crossed it to Abraham, who launched the ball over the flat-footed keeper.

The celebration was short-lived. The opposing team's captain built up a head of steam and deked his way from one end of the field to the other, sidestepped a panicked Moe and tied it up.

"Next goal wins," Vince announced, looking at his watch.

He kicked the ball back to Suzie, who did her best impression of the other captain but was stymied at the centreline by Abraham's check. Abraham scrambled back and snuck up on the skinny kid from behind while he surveyed the field and picked his pocket. He spotted Vince surging up right-field and put the ball on his foot. He gave chase.

Two defenders were back. Vince's check gave him a huge cushion. Vince stalled, headfaked and blasted past into the clear. The keeper came out to challenge. Abraham caught his check switching directions and rushed by. Vince kicked the ball. It was the perfect height — but going wide!

Abraham dug deep and sprinted hard. Leapt. The ball centimetres from his face, he butted, redirecting it past the goalie, who stood stunned with his hands in front of his chest.

The bell rang.

Vince pointed at Abraham and ran over. "That was amazing!"

The team crowded around.

"Great header, Abraham!"

"What a goal!"

"Their keeper didn't see it coming!"

Vince put his hands on Abraham's shoulders. "Why have you never played with us before?"

"Well... nobody ever asked."

"Nobody ever asked!" Vince looked at the team. "You believe that? Well I know who I'm picking every time! Three cheers for Abraham!"

"Hip-hip, hooray! Hip-hip, hooray! Hip-hip, hooray!"

"C'mon," Vince said, slinging his arm around Abraham's shoulders, "we better get to class before Mrs. P's hair turns white."

When the final bell rang, Abraham stuffed his books into his backpack.

"Taking the bus home?" Sarah asked, biting the corner of her lip.

"Yeah, I guess so."

She smiled but didn't say anything.

"Are you?"

"Yep. Do you want to... sit together?"

His heart raced. "I... sure. Yes."

"Great!" She smiled.

"Abraham." It was Mrs. P. "Before you go, can I talk to you for a moment?"

Sarah's eyes widened. "I'll save you a seat. Don't be late!" She slipped out.

"Yes, Mrs. P?"

"I was wondering" — she perched her head to the side and adjusted her glasses — "well, you see, I was really, very impressed by your report."

Abraham pulled the strap of his backpack.

"And, well, the school selects a group of special children — gifted, you might say — and a few of us teachers make it a pet project — not that we think of you as pets! No, no."

Abraham squinted. What was she getting at?

"Well let me just say it. Surely you've heard of the public speaking contest. I think — if you're interested, of course, and with your parents' permission — would you... Can I..."

"Yes, Mrs. P?"

"I don't mean to suggest you need coaching, Abraham, not at all, but ... Would you like to enter the contest, with me as your coach?"

*

The bus lurched to a stop. Abraham bent over to grab his backpack from the floor. When he sat up, Sarah handed him a piece of folded-up paper, her cheeks bright as her hair. "See you tomorrow?"

"See you tomorrow," he said, sticking the note in his pocket.

He waved to Mr. H. The door hissed closed. The horn honked twice and the kids yelled their goodbyes, the quiet neighbourhood echoing the cries.

Abraham watched the bus disappear around the corner. As he turned towards his driveway, he caught a glimpse of a curtain flutter in the window of the little brown house just up the street.

*

The smell hit his nostrils the moment he opened the front door. Tuna casserole! He dropped his bag, kicked off his sneakers and ran into the kitchen.

"Hi honey!" Mom said, turning from the stove. She knelt and Abraham hugged her.

"Tuna casserole," he whispered.

"And it's not even your birthday! It'll be ready soon. Go see your father, he's in the backyard."

Abraham put his hands against the screen door and peered through. Dad was holding a hammer and nails, a piece of plywood leaning against his thigh.

"Abraham! Perfect timing. Come out here and give me a hand, would you? Just hold that sheet up against there while I hammer it in. Perfect."

When they were done, Dad stepped back and crossed his arms. "Well, what do you think? It needs a roof still, and a door cut there, and maybe a window there."

"Is it...?"

Dad smiled and tousled Abraham's hair. "Well every knight needs a fortress. Especially one as intrepid and daring as Sir Calidas!"

"A treehouse! No way!"

"Well once we hoist it up into the crotch of the tree there, yeah... your very own treehouse!"

"But Dad..."

"Yeah?"

"Horses can't climb trees."

Dad laughed. "What do you think the hoist is for? We'll never have to worry about Okenower's wolves when we're up there!"

"It's almost as big as the king's castle!"

Dad winked. "Just wait till Princess Devada sees it."

*

Mom dished a steaming, oozing mound of casserole onto Abraham's plate.

"'I didn't lose it,' I told him, 'I know exactly where it went!' Boy did Smith bust a gut." Dad laughed, twirling the end of his fork. "I'll tell you, Smith is nothing like Johnson. Forward-thinking. Very progressive. A real team player. I think I can see a future with this company. A family man, too." He pointed his fork at Abraham. "Has a kid your age, I think."

"That's just..." — Mom dabbed her eyes — "it makes me so happy to hear that, dear. And you're not the only one with good news to share today. Right, honey?"

Abraham froze mid-chew, thinking of the note in his pocket.

"Mrs. Picadia called after school. She says she wants to coach you in the public speaking competition!"

Abraham exhaled.

"How about that!" Dad said, flinging flakes of tuna. "My kid, a public speaker! Watch out, you'll be prime minister before you know it!"

"Don't get carried away, dear. No pressure, honey. But I know you'll do great. I'm very proud of you."

Abraham wiped his smile. "And I played soccer at recess today and I scored the winning goal!"

"Well, I'll be!"

“Who is this kid?” Dad said, spraying half-chewed food. “You’re my son? An intellectual and an athlete — watch out, world!”

While Mom and Dad cleaned up, Abraham sat in Dad’s recliner, a bowl of ice cream in his lap, watching TV. The phone rang.

“Hello?” Mom said. “Abraham, it’s for you!” She shrugged and handed him the cordless phone.

“Hello? Oh, hey Vince! Yeah, ha! I still can’t believe it went in!” Mom furrowed her brow. “Uh huh. Uh huh. Well, I’d have to ask... hang on. Mom, can I join a soccer team?”

Her eyes widened and she waved her hands in front of them. “Of course you can, honey!”

When Abraham changed into his pyjamas, he remembered the note. He brought it into bed and was about to open it when Mom and Dad came in. He slid it under his pillow.

“Good night, honey,” Mom said, kissing his forehead.

“Sleep well, sire,” Dad said with a sweep of his arm. Mom slapped his shoulder and tsk’d. He winked.

“Good night, Mom. Good night, Dad.”

Mom turned off the light and closed the door.

Abraham rolled onto his stomach and slid the note out. It smelled like clean clothes. The streetlight was bright enough for him to read the bubbly handwriting. “To Abraham” it said, the M shaped like a heart. He unfolded it.

Five

"ALRIGHT GUYS, GATHER around." Coach slapped the palmed soccer ball. He had grey and black hair slicked back and thick eyebrows over kind, round eyes. The team formed a circle around him and knelt. "First off, let's give a big Wolves welcome to Abraham!"

The boys tilted their heads back and howled until they ran out of breath and started to laugh.

"Listen up!" They fell quiet. "Now you all saw what he can do out there. I wish I could tell you that you can be as good as him if you listen to what I say and practise hard. But I'm not gonna lie. Some people are just naturally talented. The best we can do is work to use that talent for the benefit of the team. Got that, Kareem?"

"Yes, Coach." He had kind, round eyes like Coach.

"Good. Now as you know—"

Kareem howled.

"Kareem. Pay attention." The boys laughed. "Listen up! As you know, the tournament is coming up, and with our dynamic duo of Abraham and Vince leading the charge—"

"Like Batman and Robin!"

"Kareem. Please. I think we've got a real good chance of—"

"Or Tom and Jerry!"

"Tom and Jerry? Kareem, what are you..." Coach shook his head. "Anyway. We've got a real good chance of making it to the finals. You all know how we do it. We've been practising hard all season. We've got the secret ingredient. We've—"

"A-1 steak sauce?"

"Seriously now, Kareem. I'm trying to — nevermind. You can bet we'll be up against the Knights in the final if not before. And you know how much I — not hate, hate is a strong word — dislike that coach of theirs. So I'm counting on you guys to bring your A game—"

"Steak sauce—"

"To give one hundred and ten percent, to come out strong and not let up till we send those Knights cowering back to their mommas. Wolves, let me hear you howl on three. One, two, three!"

Abraham tilted his head back and howled along with the other boys until he couldn't howl any more.

*

The little hand on the clock on the wall at the front of the classroom was past the 4 and Abraham was the only student in the classroom.

"Well I must say," Mrs. Picadia said, shaking her head, "I've never seen anything quite like it."

"What do you mean, Mrs. P?"

"Well not only is your speech an improvement — a vast improvement, as if that were even possible — over your report, but you've already got it memorized." She pursed her lips. "I'm just... I, well. I'm not really sure what I can do to help, Abraham."

He smiled. He felt confident, sure of himself, like he could do nothing wrong. Turning the report into a speech had been easy. The pen slid across the paper as if something — or somebody — else were controlling his hand. (It was like when he was playing soccer and his feet seemed to have minds of their own.) He didn't think too much about it. Why would he? Everything was just coming so easily to him. He was becoming who he always pictured himself to be in his head. Athletic, smart, popular. And then there was Sarah. Her notes made him feel like he'd never felt before. Just imagining her long, flowing hair—

"Abraham?"

"Uh, yes Mrs. P?"

"Why don't we start again from the beginning. I think I might be able to give you some notes on elocution."

Abraham stood up, cleared his throat and took a deep breath. He opened his lips and the words flowed from his mouth; he didn't even have to try to remember them.

*

The field was empty when Abraham stepped outside. He cinched his backpack and headed towards the fence. He crossed the street and the rumble of an engine grew louder. He looked over his shoulder. The school bus screeched to a halt and the door swung open.

"Need a lift, little man?" Mr. Hallick asked. Abraham climbed the stairs. "Grab a seat. I don't normally work this late, but I had a special request." He jerked his thumb towards the back.

Sarah, a smile on her freckled face, was the only person on the bus. Abraham's heart fluttered like laundry on a clothesline. "Sarah! What are you doing here?"

She patted the seat beside her. "I knew you had to stay late to practise your speech with Mrs. P, so I asked Mr. H if he wouldn't mind making a special trip."

"You waited...?"

"I spent some time in the library till Ms. Lamasz kicked me out. She's such a crab sometimes."

They laughed.

He reached into his pocket. "This is for you." He handed her a piece of paper folded the same way she had folded hers. Her fingers nearly touched his as she took the note and a zap passed between them.

"Oh!" she said, startled, and they laughed again. She turned the note over in her hand. "I've never seen my name written that way before. It's beautiful!"

"It's called calligraphy. It's how knights used to write poems to princesses."

She caressed the note and rested her head on his shoulder. "It's really beautiful, Abraham. I can't wait to get home and read it."

He watched the sunlight dapple the leaves of the trees lining the streets and breathed in the fresh-scented air, feeling the weight of Sarah's head on his shoulder.

"I hate to break up the canoodling," Mr. H called, "but we have arrived at your abode, Abraham."

He got lost a moment in Sarah's eyes. "Okay I gotta run. See you tomorrow!"

On the kitchen counter was a note. "Dad and I went to the movies. Dinner's in the fridge. Don't wait up! Love, Mom."

Abraham went into the backyard and climbed the rope into the treehouse. The sun was setting, lighting the sky on fire, but the only colour he saw was auburn. He smiled.

Everything was going so well. Even his parents were happy! He had everything he could ever dream of.

But Mya hadn't been in class all week. He shooed away a mosquito buzzing around his face. So what? He could always go knock on her door if he wanted to. But he had lots of friends now, anyway. What did he need her for?

The mosquito landed on his arm. He slapped it. He lifted his hand and saw blood.

Six

IT WAS RAINING on the day of the finals.

Mom and Dad stood on the sidelines in yellow raincoats and rubber boots with the parents of the other kids on the team. They cheered every time Abraham touched the ball — and even louder when he scored. When he tallied the game-winning goal in extra time in the semi-finals, Dad even howled. Mom slapped his shoulder but he didn't stop.

As Coach predicted, the Knights made it to the finals too. The rain had stopped but the field was a big puddle. It didn't matter to Abraham; he was already soaked.

"Alright team, huddle up." The boys knelt around Coach. "Let me just say it. It has been the pleasure of my coaching career seeing you boys give it your all out there today. When I started—"

"Coach, are you crying?"

"Damn it, Kareem, it's raining out. It's rain. I got rain in my eye."

"But it's not raining anymore, is it?" He held his palm up.

"Are you done Kareem? Can I get on with it?"

He blinked. "On with what?"

"With inspiring my team! With giving the big motivational speech! Nevermind. I swear Kareem, if you weren't my own flesh and blood, I'd... Anyway. Where was I..."

"'When I started,'" Kareem said. Coach looked at him. "You said, 'When I started.'"

Coach sighed. "Thank you, Kareem. When I started coaching, I never thought I'd see players as good as I'm seeing today. I never thought I'd see a team as good as I'm seeing today. You've already made me so proud—"

"Is it raining again?"

"So proud... that even if we take home the first losers — sorry, second place trophy today, I'll still be proud. But if you boys dig deep, and you give one hundred and twenty percent, and you show those Knights what a pack of thirsty, hungry, worn-out, rained-on, soaked-to-the-bone Wolves can do, you can win this — and I'll buy you all the pizza you can eat, because man I hate those Knights! Now Wolves, let me hear you howl!"

The howl erupted from their mouths. The parents howled too.

The referee blew the whistle. The boys sloshed onto the field.

"Abraham," Coach said. "We're counting on you."

"Let's go Abraham!" Mom and Dad yelled.

He looked at them and smiled. Standing beside them in a shiny purple raincoat, eyes shimmering, was Mya.

*

The whistle blew. “Time out, Wolves,” the ref said.

Abraham hustled over to the sidelines, his team trudging behind.

“Huddle up, huddle up,” Coach said, running his hand down his face. The boys knelt. “Okay. I knew this game was going to be exciting, but I didn’t think it was going to be this exciting. It’s been a long day. We’re down to the last couple minutes. I know we’re all tired and cold, but we can do this. We just need one goal. One goal, and we can all go to the Pizza Palace to dry off, warm up and stuff our faces with some pizza. Does that sound good, Wolves?”

“Dad, I’m cold.”

“Not now, Kareem. I said, does that sound good, Wolves?”

Silence.

Abraham stood up. “Mind if I say something, Coach?”

“No no, go right ahead.” Coach buried his hands in his pockets.

Abraham looked each of his teammates in the eyes. They were shivering, staring at the ground, arms wrapped around themselves. “Who wants to quit right now?”

“Woah, woah!” Coach said, waving his hands. “I didn’t say anything about quitting.”

Abraham held his hand up. Coach quieted. “I know you’re tired. I know you’re cold. I know you want nothing more than to go home, change into pyjamas and sip hot chocolate in front of the TV for the rest of the night.”

"Mmm, hot chocolate!"

"Kareem, please. And you know what? We can do that. We could quit right now and walk off the field. And our moms and our dads would take us home, because this is a game, and we don't have to play if we don't want to. And you know what?

"What?" Kareem said.

"I don't want to quit."

"Why?" Kareem asked.

"Because I know that If I go home now and get into my PJs and sip cocoa, I'll remember that instead of choosing to play, and possibly winning, I chose to quit. The next day, and the day after that, and the day after that, I would wonder what if — what if we had played the game? And what if... We had won? Vince." Vince lifted his head. "Do you want to quit?"

"No."

"Joon." Joon uncrossed his arms. "Do you want to quit?"

"No!"

"Kareem. Do you want to quit?"

He looked from Abraham to Coach — "Don't even think about it," Coach whispered — and back to Abraham. He stomped his foot, splashing water over his teammates' shoes. "No!"

"Then you know what, Wolves?"

"What?" they shouted.

"We're not going to quit!" Abraham stomped the ground. "We're going to play! And we're going to win!"

The boys stomped their feet, tilted their heads back and howled.

Abraham led the Wolves onto the field. The ref blew the whistle and handed the ball to a Knight. He lobbed it to an open winger who played it back to the defence. The Wolves fell into a defensive trap, luring the Knights forward. The defenceman kicked it to his partner who booted it to midfield. The Wolves read the play and adjusted their zone.

The midfielder trotted towards the centreline and the trap closed around him. Spotting the winger with some space around him, he paused to tee up the cross. Kareem seized the opportunity and pounced. Panicking, the midfielder misfired and caught as much turf as ball. The ball fluttered, tailing a spray of puddle water, and fell short of the intended receiver who lurched forward to cut the distance. Vince had a leg up and beat him to the ball. He planted his foot on it and pulled back. The winger over-committed, slipped and fell. Vince broke into a run and the Wolves prowled upfield. The red-faced winger regained his footing and chased Vince with a full head of steam.

"Man on!" Abraham yelled.

Vince glanced over his shoulder, jerked left, tapped the ball right and came to a standstill as the Knight circled around him.

"Open!" Abraham called.

Vince centred the ball and Joon kicked it on the run. The ball sailed over Abraham's right shoulder, dripping wet like a rainy meteorite, and landed in a puddle. The Knights defenceman slide-checked in a desperate attempt to stymy

Abraham's advance but overestimated the slickness of the grass and overshot his mark. Abraham hopped and cleared the horizontal defender, landing with a torrential splash, and collected the ball and hit his stride. The other defender closed in and the keeper crept forward to cut off the angle.

Abraham was all alone.

"Take the shot!" Vince shouted.

The defenceman neared. Abraham avoided his sliding tackle with a deft flip of his toe. The keeper reached the edge of the box, feet stuttering, arms outstretched.

"Shoot!" Coach screamed.

It was just Abraham and the keeper.

Then, out the corner of his eye, he saw Vince attack the net. Abraham swiped the ball and it sailed, spinning, towards him. The goalie scrambled, sprinting to defend the opposite side. With a single tap, Vince returned the volley. The keeper slid, dug in and darted back, but it was too late. Abraham wound up and one-timed it, burying the ball in the top corner.

The crowd erupted. Vince pumped his fist and ran towards Abraham.

"That's what I'm talking about!" Coach yelled.

"Abra-ham! Abra-ham!" Mom and Dad chanted, the other parents joining in.

The Wolves encircled him and hoisted him up on their shoulders, cheering and howling as they ran around the field — until Kareem slipped and they collapsed into a laughing, soaking-wet pile.

*

Abraham sat at the head of the table at Pizza Palace.

"Another slice of ham and pineapple, Abraham?"

"Abraham, you want more soda?"

"Pass Abraham some more chicken wings!"

"Excuse me, can we please have some more ranch dressing?"

The neon-lit room was overrun by the Wolves, who were kneeling on chairs, spilling drinks and strewing chicken bones, pizza crusts and used napkins across the long table.

Coach whistled with his fingers and they went quiet. Their eyes fell on the shining silver soccer ball-shaped trophy on the table in front of him.

"Well boys? What can I say. We did it!" They howled. Coach laughed. "Now hold up. I don't wanna talk too long because I know you boys are hungry, and I don't want you chewing my face off, but I got something to say."

"What is it, Dad?"

"Just hold on a minute and I'll tell you, Kareem. Man. What I want to say is... Damn it felt good to beat those Knights!"

The boys howled and beat their fists on the table.

"Hold up, hold up. Easy on the furniture there, boys. I'm paying for the pizza, not for the repairs. You think I make money coaching boys' soccer? Anyway, I'll let you get back to feeding your faces, but first I wanna say this: We couldn't have done this if we didn't play as a team. But there's one player who deserves special recognition."

"Who is it, Dad?"

"Not you, Kareem." Coach lifted the trophy. "Come over here and take this, Abraham. You earned it."

The boys howled. Abraham stood up. He felt like he'd grown a foot taller. They patted his back as he walked around the table.

"Here you go," Coach said. "Take good care of it and keep it as long as you like. But give it back when you're done with it. I wanna bask in the glory of whoopin' those Knights for a while too."

Abraham wrapped his hands around the base of the trophy and raised it into the air.

"Abra-ham! Abra-ham!" the boys chanted.

That's when he saw Mya sitting by herself at the counter.

*

"Wow, cool car, Mr. Johnson!" Abraham said, clutching the trophy as he slid across the black leather seat.

"Keep playing the way you did today," Mr. Johnson said, steel blue eyes staring at Abraham in the rearview mirror, "and you'll have one of your own someday. Seat warmers, boys? Vince told me you were good, but not that good. What team did you come over from?"

Abraham buckled up. "The Wolves are my first team, sir."

"New to the game, huh? Impressive. I bet your parents are proud."

Abraham smiled at the shining trophy. "Yeah, I guess they are."

"I'll tell you, I'm sure proud of Vince. Passing you the ball back when he could have taken the shot himself — well, that's pure class. You can't teach a move like that." Vince smiled. The car entered a tunnel, and the trophy stopped shining. "But soccer's a team sport, just like everything else. Somebody has to make the passes, and somebody has to take the shots. And if my work is any indication, the world could sure use some more shot-takers." Mr. Johnson's steely gaze found Abraham again. "What'd you say your last name was?"

Abraham told him. The trophy gleamed as the car passed under a streetlight.

"Hmm, that's right." Mr. Johnson snapped his finger. "I thought I recognized your old man at the field. Hard to tell with that bright yellow get-up he was wearing. I'd only seen him in a shirt and tie before."

Abraham's eyes widened. He remembered when Dad had come home angry that day. Mr. Johnson was—

"A real shot-taker, just like your old man. I was sorry to see him go." He pulled the car to the curb. He snaked his arm around the passenger seat and looked back. "This is you, isn't it?"

"Thanks for the lift, Mr. Johnson!" Abraham said, sliding out.

"No problem at all." Mr. Johnson smiled, flashing his canine teeth. "Say hi to your old man for me."

Seven

"COME ON OUT," Mom said from the living room. "Let's see you!"

Abraham took a deep breath and stepped out of his room.

"Oh you look so cute in your little bowtie!"

"A real dapper dude," Dad said. "I bet if I looked like that on our first date, I would have gotten to first base a lot sooner."

Mom slapped his arm. "Never mind your father. The important thing is that you have a good time." She fussed with Abraham's tie and straightened his collar.

"Mom," he said, squirming.

"Don't be nervous." She picked a piece of fluff off his shoulder.

"Mom!"

"Sorry, honey. Okay. I'm sure Sarah's parents will love you." She stood back and smiled. "How couldn't they?"

“Play your cards right,” Dad said, putting on a coat, “and you and me will be running Sarah’s dad’s company in no time!”

“Dear!” Mom said. “You didn’t tell me Sarah’s dad was your boss!”

“He sure is. Small world, huh? Don’t worry, Abraham. Smith knows Johnson is sniffing around again, so he’ll do anything to keep me happy.” He grabbed the car keys.

“Honey,” Mom said, kneeling. “Don’t worry about any of that. Just have fun, okay?” She kissed Abraham’s cheek.

*

Dad drove off. Abraham glanced at the decorative pond and climbed the steps to the immense wooden doors. The knocker looked like a golden lion. He grabbed it and rapped twice.

A small shutter slid open above his head and two eyes appeared. “Who goes there?” asked a high-pitched voice.

“Oh, hi!” He stood on his tiptoes. “I’m Abraham.”

The eyes glanced down. “Ah yes. Here to see the fair Sarah, are you not?”

Abraham stifled a laugh. “Indeed I am, with your leave.” He bowed his head.

“Ahh, I knew not that it would be a gentlemanly squire calling this afternoon.” The shutter slid shut. Chains clinked, bolts clicked and a latch snapped. The door creaked open.

There stood a bald-headed old man in red-and-blue livery, one arm across his front and the other across his back. He bowed.

"Welcome," he said, straightening. "I am Rupert, the butler. May I take your coat and put those" — he pointed to the flowers Abraham was holding — "in a vase with water? Ms. Sarah will be down shortly."

He swept his arm, revealing a grand spiral staircase twisting from the middle of the foyer to the second floor. A glass dome in the ceiling let in the afternoon sunlight.

Abraham had never seen anything so majestic. He sat on a cushioned bench beside the door and untied his shoes.

"Abraham?" Sarah stood at the top of the stairs, a hand upon the balustrade. She wore a simple white summer dress and a single yellow marigold in her hair. Abraham stood up and watched her descend the staircase, feeling as if it were a dream.

"From the young suitor," Rupert said, handing Sarah a vase with the marigolds.

"Oh Abraham! They're beautiful. Let's show them to Mom and Dad. And introduce you, of course." She slid her arm through Abraham's and led him behind Rupert, who pushed open the doors to the left of the entrance.

A log fire was roaring in a huge hearth. Two tall wood and leather chairs faced it. From them rose a man — thick grey hair, smooth skin and calm, tired eyes — and a woman who looked like a grown-up Sarah.

"You must be Abraham!" the woman said, approaching.

"Look at the flowers he brought, Mom!"

"Marigolds! How'd he know?"

The man extended a hand, gold rings decorating his fingers. "Nice to meet you, young man."

Abraham shook his hand. "Pleased to meet you, Mr. Smith. And you, Mrs. Smith! Thank you for inviting me into your home. And what a home!"

Mrs. Smith laughed, lifting her chin.

"We are content with our little palace, as we like to call it. You're welcome. Anyway, I'm sure you two don't want to spend all afternoon talking to us old fuddy-duddies—"

"Oh, Dad."

"Now, now, Sarah. Run along and play. Rupert will fetch you when it's suppertime."

"Can I show Abraham the attic?"

"Whatever you like, dear. Just be careful in the gallery."

Sarah grabbed Abraham's hand and tugged. "See you at dinner!" he said, letting himself be dragged away. "You have an art gallery?"

Sarah giggled, a glimmer in her eyes. "Want to play hide-and-seek?"

"Uh huh! You'll probably win though. I bet you know all the hiding spots."

"Sure do! Why don't you go hide first? Just to be nice, I'll count to 75."

"Deal!"

"Ready... set... go!" She covered her eyes. "One... two... three..."

Abraham bounded up the spiral stairs two at a time and darted down the hallway. There were identical doors one after another on both sides of the hall and a single door at the end. Paintings of people in old clothes hung on the walls in between. He opened the nearest door on the right and looked in.

Rolls of fabric in different colours and patterns leaned against the wooden walls. A sewing machine and chair stood near the window overlooking the front yard. He closed the door and scurried across the hallway.

The next room was twice as wide as the last, with a checkered wooden floor and two full suits of armour standing against the back wall between two huge windows that peered out into the sloping, well-manicured backyard. Each suit of armour was holding a wooden lance, just like the ones knights used for jousting. A rack was affixed to the wall on his left loaded with long, narrow metal blades. A fencing room? He shook his head and closed the door.

He ran to the second-last door on the right and opened it. It smelled like dust. The curtains were shut but he could see that everything in the room was covered with a sheet. He went in, closed the door and couldn't see a thing. He fumbled around with his hands out in front of him.

He touched a sheet; there was something cold and hard behind it. He tugged the sheet and it fell over his head to the ground. Careful not to trip on it, he took a few steps away.

He stopped walking and stood very still. Seventy-five seconds had to be up by now, he thought.

He listened to himself breathe. He heard footsteps in the hallway. A door opened and closed. More footsteps.

Another door opened and closed. The footsteps moved away, stopped. Sarah giggled. The footsteps came closer. The door opened.

"Hmmm… I wonder if Abraham's in here."

He stifled a laugh. The light clicked on and he held his breath.

"That's funny. I don't remember that statue's sheet coming off."

The footsteps came close.

"Or seeing that one before!"

Closer.

"It's much shorter than the others."

His breath was running out.

"I wonder what it looks like."

Closest.

Slowly, a corner of the sheet lifted. He couldn't hold his breath any longer. "Boo!" he yelled, throwing his arms up.

She shrieked and giggled. "Found you!"

"Good thing, too. I almost ran out of breath!" He looked at the statue he'd pulled the sheet off. "Is that a …?"

"Daddy calls it a monolith. He had it imported from—"

"England! Druids used them to measure the positions of the stars."

"That's right. Of course you knew that. You're so smart." She dropped the sheet and stepped towards him, her eyes gleaming.

He took a step back. "Sarah?"

"Yes, Abraham?" She took another step towards him.

He stepped back. "What are you doing?"

She stepped forward. "I won, didn't I?"

He stepped back and felt the cold, hard stone at his back. "Uh huh."

She stepped forward. "Don't I deserve a prize?"

"Sarah, I've never—" He pushed against the monolith.

"Shhh..." She leaned forward, eyes closed.

"What if your mom or dad or—" The stone rocked backwards slightly.

"Ms. Sarah?" Rupert was standing at the door.

She turned. "Huh?"

Abraham heard a creaking noise. The stone! He grabbed Sarah's shoulders and dove, pulling her with him.

"Dear god, no!" Rupert exclaimed.

A shadow blocked out the light. Sarah screamed and the house shook as the stone thundered to the floor.

*

"Are you okay?" Abraham asked.

"My leg..." Sarah whimpered.

It was caught under the monolith! "Rupert! Get help!"

"Yes, m'lord."

"It hurts!" she whined.

"Hold on!" Abraham said. He ran out and to the other end of the hallway, threw open the door, grabbed one of the lances and dragged it back.

"What are you doing?" Sarah cried.

"Don't worry, I'll get you out of there!"

He ran back out and down the hall, threw open another door, grabbed a roll of fabric and dragged it back.

"Sarah!" Mrs. Smith shrieked, coming into the room. Mr. Smith was right behind her.

Abraham placed the roll of fabric perpendicular to the monolith.

"Hurry, Abraham, it hurts!"

Mrs. Smith knelt beside Sarah and held her hand.

"Just another minute!" He placed the lance across the roll and positioned the tip under the stone near her leg.

"Mr. Smith, I need you to push down on the lance. Sarah, when you feel it lift, pull your leg out and roll out of the way!"

Mr. Smith got down on his knees and placed his hands on the lance.

Abraham grabbed hold of the stone. "Now!"

Mr. Smith's face turned red as he pressed down. Abraham lifted as hard as he could.

"It's moving!" Mrs. Smith said. Sarah screamed. "A little more!"

Mr. Smith yelled. Abraham pulled, his fingers, hands, arms, back and neck straining.

Sarah shrieked and rolled free.

"There!" Mrs. Smith said.

Abraham pulled his fingers away. Mr. Smith fell back onto the floor. The stone settled with a thud.

Rupert stood at the door holding a crowbar. "The ambulance" — he hid it behind his back — "shall be arriving anon."

*

The paramedics rolled the stretcher to the back of the ambulance, its red and white lights screaming in silence. Sarah, propped up by a pillow, waved at Abraham, who was standing between Mr. Smith and Rupert on the porch. He waved back. Mrs. Smith, smiling grimly, stepped into the ambulance and sat across from her daughter. The paramedics closed the doors and the ambulance rolled away.

"The young man's father has been sent for," Rupert said.

"Before he arrives," Mr. Smith said, "I'd like to have a word with you in my study. Rupert?"

The butler skipped ahead and opened the doors.

"Please." Mr. Smith pointed to the chairs in front of the fire. They sat and Abraham stared into the flames. "When I was a boy, not much older than you are now, I was caught in a situation that gives me pause to this day."

Abraham shifted in his seat.

"I believe the choices we make in moments when we must act without thinking are the most revealing of who we are as people." He turned his head towards Abraham. "Rupert told me what he saw before the incident."

Abraham opened his mouth to speak.

"Ah! Please, just listen. In my youth, as I said, I was in a similar situation. But unable — unwilling, rather — to resist, I made a decision with far-reaching and damaging consequences. I will say no more about it than that, except that as the father of a girl the same age as she was, I wished — wish! — I had comported myself as you did today."

"But Mr. Smith," Sarah's father faced the fire, ringed fingers tented together, "if I hadn't pushed the monolith, it—"

"And if I had had it properly anchored, you wouldn't have been able to topple it. No, Abraham, I've been over this in my head a thousand times already. I blame nobody, except perhaps myself."

Abraham sat back in the chair and watched the flickering flames.

"And if it wasn't for your quick thinking, Sarah's injury, as severe as it is, would have been far more grave." He glanced at Abraham, eyes twinkling in the firelight. "A lever and a fulcrum using a lance and a roll of fabric." His chest rose and fell. "Simply marvellous. Ingenious, really. Abraham, I — no, we; the entire Smith family — are in your debt. If there is ever anything — anything! — we can do, please do not hesitate to ask."

There was a gentle rap at the door.

"Yes?"

"M'lord," Rupert said. "A Mr." — he said Abraham's last name — "is here to retrieve the young man."

Mr. Smith repeated the name, eyes widening as he stared at Abraham. "You didn't tell me you were his boy! Rupert, invite him in, and fetch the decanter and two glasses. And don't take no for an answer!"

*

Abraham buckled his seatbelt. The engine sputtered and caught.

"Well you sure made an impression on old Smith," Dad said, slapping the steering wheel.

Abraham looked out the window, watching the houses pass. "I thought I was in for it, for sure."

"For trying to smooch his daughter?" Dad winked. Abraham shook his head. "Or for knocking over his druid's rock?"

"Monolith, Dad."

"Whatever it's called, I'm just happy it didn't break. No way I would have been able to repay him for that!"

It was dark but the houses in the neighbourhood were lit up from the inside. Shadows crept on the walls.

"Something on your mind, son?"

"It's weird, that's all."

"What's that?"

"It just seems like everything is working out for the best."

Dad turned the wheel. "What's wrong with that?"

The curtains were drawn at the one-storey brown house. Dad pulled the car into their driveway.

"Nothing, I guess."

Eight

THE MASTER OF CEREMONIES stepped up to the microphone.

"The next con—" The speakers screeched. He pulled back, his upper lip curling. The screeching died down. "The next contestant is from Mrs. Picadia's class. Here to talk about" — he looked at a cue card — "Indian culture is Abraham. Abraham!" He clapped and walked out of the spotlight.

Applause washed over Abraham like a wave. He stood from his seat at the back of the stage and stepped into the spotlight and up to the mic. The applause stopped and there was only silence. He peered out into the darkness. Mom waved, elbowing Dad, who gave the thumbs up. A few rows closer, Mrs. Picadia pushed her glasses up the bridge of her nose with the back of her wrist.

Abraham looked at the table stage-left and the three shadowy faces behind it.

"Esteemed judges," he said, lifting his hand towards them, "fellow contestants," waving it back, "and respected audience," aiming it forward, palm open to the ceiling. "Today, I would like to tell you a story. It is an old story, and you may have heard it told before." He paused. "But" — he raised his index finger — "you have never heard it told quite like this..."

And just like that, the words of the speech began to flow from Abraham's mouth just as they had each time he'd practised it. But this time — as syllable led to syllable, word led to word, and sentence led to sentence — he became aware of more.

He became aware of the intricate convolutions of his tongue, jaw and lips. He became aware of the indeliberate, inexplicable prestidigitations of his fingers. He became aware of the stage hard beneath his soles, the light hot on his crown, the movement of the air around, in, out and through him.

The words flowed out, and he became aware of the audience's attention grasping and clinging to his intangible utterances. He became aware of their seats creaking as they inched closer to the edges. He became aware of their quick, hushed breaths growing shallower and shallower to hear each and every susurrant, sibilant, plosive sound that escaped his lips.

He became aware of the floating, swirling, dancing dust motes illuminated on the stage in front of him. He became aware of the ticking of some invisible, ethereal clock — now fast, now slow — keeping track of a time that passed, returned, advanced, retreated, approached and receded in a realm beyond the phenomenal, beyond the numinal, a time that reached back, back, back to before consciousness decided to blink itself into existence.

"And to this day," he heard himself say, "we've forgotten who we are. And so we spend our lives, our entire lives, trying to remember — and trying to find ourselves."

And finally — as the spell broke and the claps erupted into a tsunami of applause and Mom and Dad and Mrs. P rose from their seats and everyone else did too, even the judges — Abraham became aware of Mya, standing way at the back of the auditorium, holding a doll with brown hair and brown eyes and a little polka dot bowtie that looked exactly like his.

Nine

"OPEN MINE NEXT!"

"No, mine!"

"Open mine, Abraham, mine!"

"Ryan," Abraham said.

Ryan pointed at himself. "Me?"

"Yeah! Bring it over!"

The crowd of kids jostling in front of the living room couch, where Abraham was sitting beside Sarah with a cast on her leg, parted to let Ryan through. He carried his parcel in both hands and held it out. "Happy birthday, Abraham."

"What is it?"

"I bet it's Lego!"

"No way, you dummy! It'd be bigger than that if it was Lego."

"Says who?"

Mom brandished the instant camera. "Smile!" Abraham put his arm around Ryan. The flash popped.

"You wanna help me open it?" Abraham asked Sarah.

"Sure!"

She pulled the ribbon off. Abraham tore at the paper. "Oh cool!"

"What is it? What is it?"

"I can't see!"

"Let me see!"

Abraham held the gift up.

"Oh no way!"

"Cool!"

"I told you it wasn't Lego!"

"Thanks Ryan," Abraham said, slugging his shoulder. Ryan shrugged and smiled sheepishly.

"Here you go, birthday boy!" Sarah put the ribbon on Abraham's head. Everyone laughed.

"Food's ready!" Mom called from the kitchen. "Come grab a plate and help yourself."

Abraham waited till everyone else went. The table was still loaded. Tuna casserole, shells and dogs, ham and pineapple pizza. He filled his plate and brought it back to his seat.

Every chair in the house was full. Some kids had to sit on the floor. The Wolves were all there, and everybody from Abraham's class — except Mya.

When they were done eating, Dad called them out to the backyard. It was sunny and warm. He had set up the sprinkler and the Slip 'n Slide and decorated the treehouse like a pirate ship. A horse-shaped piñata hung from the rope.

Mom gave everyone a turn with the piñata. She put a blind fold on them, handed them a hockey stick and spun them around till they couldn't walk straight. Ryan threw up and Mom called his parents to come get him. Kareem stumbled the wrong way and swung at the other kids until Coach yelled at him and he stopped. Vince wound up and hit it like a homerun, exploding lollipops and gold coins everywhere.

Dad was chasing kids around with the hose when Mom came outside with a giant birthday cake shaped like a knight on a horse. Everyone sang Happy Birthday. Abraham took a deep breath and blew out every candle except one. He looked at Sarah and everyone went "Oooh!" One of the candles sputtered back to life. "What the heck!" Abraham said. Then another. Then another. He, Sarah and Vince all had to blow to make the candles go out and stay out.

Way too soon, parents came by to pick up their kids. Abraham stood by the front door to give out goodie bags and say goodbye.

"Happy birthday, Abraham," Coach said. He leaned close. "Say, you almost done with that trophy?"

"I'll bring it by soon, I promise. Oh, Coach?"

"Yeah?"

"How come Mya didn't come?"

"Oh you know. Girls and their dolls."

When Mr. Smith came to the door, Dad invited him in. "Why don't you take Sarah to the treehouse?" he said to Abraham. "We won't be long."

"How am I supposed to get up there with this thing on?" She pointed at her cast.

Dad shrugged. "Abraham can get a horse up there. I'm sure he can manage a girl."

"Dear!"

*

Abraham clambered up the tree and leaned over the railing. "Just put your foot in the loop and I'll hoist you up. No, not that foot — your good one! You ready?"

"Yup!"

"Okay, hold on!" He pulled on the rope and felt it lift.

"Woah!"

He pulled again and again till he saw Sarah's hair then her face. He tied off and opened the door. "Welcome to my humble abode," he said with a bow.

"Much obliged." Sarah curtsied. She lost her balance but Abraham reached out and steadied her. She giggled, brushing the hair from her face. "My knight in shining armour."

He rolled his eyes. "Yeah, right. You wouldn't be in that thing if it weren't for me." He leaned against the railing and looked out at the sunset.

"You know that wasn't your fault." She stood beside him. "Daddy said so. Anyways, it could be worse. I'll be out of this thing and ready to play hide-and-seek again before you know it."

He laughed. "I think I'll let you hide first this time."

She put her head on his shoulder. He watched the sun drop lower and lower, hoping it wouldn't just this once.

"So what'd you wish for?"

"Isn't it obvious?"

"What do you mean?"

"Well, one of the candles didn't go out. You know what that means, don't you?"

"Yeah — but then three candles lit up again!"

"Yeah, that was funny."

"Abraham?" She faced him.

"Yeah?"

"Happy birthday." She moved her lips towards his and they touched and Abraham felt fireworks go off inside.

"Sarah!" Mr. Smith called. "Time to go!"

They looked at each other and smiled. He hoisted her down and escorted her to the front door.

With serious looks on their faces, Dad and Mr. Smith shook hands and nodded at each other.

Abraham waved as they drove off, Sarah's auburn tresses blowing out the window. The fireworks inside extinguished and floated back down to earth.

"What a day, huh?" Dad said, leaning against the doorframe.

"What a day."

Ten

ABRAHAM PULLED THE HOOD over his head and looked up and down the rainy street.

He hoisted the trophy and held it close so it wouldn't get wet. A car sped up behind him. He stopped off the sidewalk onto a lawn. The car blasted past, sending a puddle soaring in a wave of wet that just missed him. He looked back and hurried on.

The curtains were drawn in the windows of the little brown house. The bare lightbulb over the porch was off. He put the trophy down on the splintered deck and pulled back his hood. He knocked. The knocks echoed.

He waited, feeling like he was being watched. Thunder rumbled, low and menacing, like the growl of a big dog.

The porch light blinked on. Metal squeaked and the door opened. And there was Mya.

"Hi!" Abraham said.

"Yes?" She looked pale, her eyes dull and far away.

"I... uh..." — he pointed to the trophy — "came to bring this to Coach. To your dad."

"He's not here. Is that all?"

Was she mad at him? "Well, I — You haven't been at school lately. Are you okay?"

She blinked once, slowly. "Yes, I'm fine. Thank you for asking."

"Okay good, because I was — well I wouldn't say worried, but I've been wanting to talk to you about... about... you know, but you haven't been at school, and Mrs. P didn't know anything, and—"

Thunder rumbled and lightning flashed in her eyes. "Would you like to come in?" She stepped back and the door creaked open.

"I shouldn't stay long, my mom and dad..." He stepped inside and shrugged off his coat.

Mya turned and disappeared around the corner of the hallway. Lightning illuminated the edges of the curtains. He tiptoed along the dusty floor. The hallway was empty.

"Mya?"

A spider dropped on its invisible string and spun around in front of his face. He stepped around it, the floorboards creaking underfoot.

"Mya?"

"Down here." Her voice was muffled — and came from behind him.

He looked at the floor and saw a faint outline. A trapdoor! "Mya?"

"Stand back!"

The floor opened, hinging away from him, and slammed open. A puff of dust rose like smoke.

He squinted into the darkness and saw a ladder. He turned around and stepped backwards onto the top rung.

Down and down he went.

The darkness gradually lightened into purple.

His foot touched the floor. He looked up. The trapdoor was a stamp-sized hole at the top of the ladder. The light went out.

He felt a breeze on the back of his neck and shivered. He turned around. Where was she?

The purple light was coming from far away. He walked towards it, his footsteps hollow thuds on the cold, hard ground. The light got brighter. He shivered again.

"Mya?"

The purple light rushed at him, pulsing and expanding as it neared. He looked down; his legs carried him forward. The light shot at his face, brightening to indigo, pink, rose, white. He was enveloped.

"Mya!" he yelled. It sounded like a thought.

"Hello, Abraham." It didn't sound like Mya but he knew it was. "Are you having fun?"

"I'm scared."

A laugh rippled through his mind and the fear was gone.

"How about now?"

"Where am I?"

"Where you always were."

"This doesn't look like Rivertide."

"I don't mean Rivertide, silly."

"Then what do you mean?"

"You are where you always were."

"Where's that?"

"Here."

"Where's here?"

"Just here."

The light blinked off. Lightning flashed, brightening the unfinished basement. Abraham saw a sink, a washing machine and a dryer. A window looked out onto the grass where rain fell in puddles.

"Mya!"

"Yes?"

He turned around. She was holding a doll and kneeling on a circular blue rug. A glass globe hung from an arched lampstand, casting rays of light around her. She was surrounded by dioramas. One looked like his backyard, with a treehouse and the rope hanging from it. Another looked like his living room. Sitting on a small couch watching a tiny TV were dolls that looked like Mom and Dad. Another diorama looked like Mrs. P's classroom, another one the soccer field — each was filled with dolls that resembled his classmates and teammates. Another diorama had a spiral staircase; another, two suits of armour holding lances; another was filled with little statues.

"Mya," he whispered, "what is all this?"

She smiled. In one hand she held the brown-haired, brown-eyed doll with the polka dot bowtie; in the other, a doll with freckles and long, wavy reddish-brown hair.

Mya's eyes shimmered. "Well, what do you think? Isn't it the most wonderful game?"

It hit him like a flash of lightning. He swallowed. "This... this is all a game?"

"Uh huh!"

"The finals... the public speaking competition... my birthday?"

"Of course, silly!"

"... Sarah?"

"Yup!"

His shoulders sagged. He couldn't believe it. It was all a game? He looked at his feet. He wanted to get out. He wanted to run, fast and far. But how? Where?

"Oh." She shook her head. "Oh no. You didn't know this was the game? You thought... you thought it was... real?"

He shifted his weight from one leg to the other. It wasn't real? None of it?

She stood up and took a step towards him.

"Don't."

She reached out a hand.

His eyes shot up. "Don't!"

Her hand dropped. "I thought you knew. I thought you knew it was a game."

"So the whole time, the whole time you weren't in school... you were here, playing with these dolls, messing up our lives?"

"Messing up?" She stepped back. "Abraham, I thought you knew! I thought we were playing... together!"

He turned away.

"Why do you think I smiled or winked whenever I saw you? I thought you — I thought we — were having fun!"

"Fun." He shook his head, a teardrop falling from his cheek.

"Oh, Abraham. I'm sorry."

He wiped his face with the back of his hand. "It's ... no. No. It's not okay. You can't just play games with people's lives like that! People aren't just dolls for you to play with — we're real people! With real feelings! And what we say and what we do matters!"

She flashed a smile.

"What's so funny?"

"'We.'"

"Huh?"

"You said 'we'."

"Yeah, so?"

"Oh Abraham, you really don't understand, do you?" She sat on the rug and picked up the doll that looked like him. She straightened its bowtie and smoothed its hair.

"No," he said, tears falling. "No, I don't understand."

"In this game," she said to the doll, "there are only two players: you and me." She pulled back the tiny sheet on the small bed in the diorama that looked like his bedroom. "And the only person's life we're playing with," she tucked the doll into the bed, "you and I are playing with, that is," — she looked at Abraham — "is yours."

"I don't want to play anymore."

She frowned. "Why not? Aren't you having fun?"

"Well... yes."

"Don't you like having friends, winning at soccer, and" — she smiled — "kissing Sarah?"

His eyes widened. "You... you did that too?"

"No, Abraham, you did it. You wanted it, and it happened. I just helped. It's that simple, really."

He wiped his cheeks. "I don't want your help anymore."

"What do you mean?"

He stepped forward. "I don't want to play your game anymore!"

"But we're having so much fun! You said so yourself."

He knelt beside the small bed. "Oh, I'm having fun alright. But if the people I'm having fun with aren't choosing to have fun with me — if you're choosing for them — then it's not really them, is it?" He reached for the doll.

"What are you doing?"

He grabbed it and pulled back before she could snatch it.

"Don't touch that!" she shrieked. "That's mine!"

"I don't want to play your game anymore, Mya." He stood, clutching the doll.

"Give it back."

"Or what? You'll tell on me?"

"Give it back, Abraham. The game doesn't have to end this way."

He held the doll in his hand, straightened its bowtie, smoothed its hair. "I think you've had enough fun, Mya." He wrapped one hand around its torso, the other around its legs. "I don't want to play anymore." He twisted.

"Wait." A tear shone in the corner of her eye.

His fingers slackened. "Why?"

"Please."

He loosened his grip.

"It's not just a game. These dolls... they mean so much more to me than you could know. Ever since my mother died..." She hung her head and a sob racked her body.

He dropped his hands. "Mya, I'm sorry—"

"Since my mother died" — she sniffled and raised her head, looking at him with jewel-encrusted eyes — "I haven't had anyone to play with. I've been so sad and lonely. It's not easy to make friends, when..." She choked up and sobbed again.

"Oh Mya," he said, putting his arms around her. "I'm so sorry."

She sniffled and lay her head on his shoulder. "It's not easy to make friends when... when... when I'm afraid they'll die, just like she did." She wailed.

He held her until her cries quieted and her body stopped shaking. "I'm sorry, Mya."

She wiped her cheeks. "It's okay."

"No," he said, holding up the doll and tightening his grip. "I'm sorry for this." He twisted and pulled, the fibres of the doll tearing and snapping apart. "But I. Don't. Want. To. Play. Any. More!"

Mya screamed.

*

Abraham was outside in the rain, halfway home, when he realized where he was. The torn ends of the doll were in his hands. He stuffed them into his jacket pockets.

Abraham opened the front door. It smelled like pee. He knew what that meant: fried livers for dinner. He dropped his jacket on the floor.

Mom and Dad were already sitting down and eating.

"Oh, there you are," Mom said.

"Dig in before it gets cold," Dad said.

Abraham pushed the blackened fleshy-pink chunks around his plate.

"Something wrong, honey?"

"No, I just... I'm not hungry."

"The more for the rest of us." Dad grabbed Abraham's plate and scooped the chunks onto his.

Abraham listened to the clatter of cutlery and the smacking of lips. "May I please be excused?"

"No, I think you should stay for a while," Mom said. "Dinner time is family time, after all. Was Coach happy to get his trophy back?"

Abraham furrowed his brow. He'd forgotten why he went to Mya's house.

"You'll need to win another one to fill the space on your shelf," Dad said, cramming in another mouthful.

"Playing games isn't all about winning trophies though, honey. Sometimes the best competition a person can have is with himself."

Dad coughed. “Who said that?”

“You know what? I don’t remember.”

“Somebody who never won a lot of trophies I bet!”

“Can I have some ice cream?” Abraham asked.

“You know the rules, honey. No dinner means no dessert.”

“But I had ice cream for dinner—”

“Abraham,” Dad said, spitting a fleck of liver, “those are the rules. Now your mom spent a lot of time making you dinner. And just because you don’t feel like eating it doesn’t mean you can go and eat whatever you want instead. You can’t just do what you want and expect people to let you. That’s not how the world works.”

Abraham sighed. “Can I be excused now, please?”

“Go ahead, honey.”

He pushed his chair back.

“But don’t even think about turning on that TV!”

He went downstairs and flicked on the light in the basement. His toys were right where he had left them.

Eleven

ABRAHAM WAS STANDING OUTSIDE when the school bus rounded the corner. It spewed smoke, grumbling, as it neared. It sped by. He chased after. It squealed to a halt a couple driveways down. The door swung open.

Mr. Hallick shook his head, grinning. "Sorry about that, little man. Haven't had my coffee today."

The bus lurched forward.

Abraham walked down the aisle. Nobody said hi or good morning. Sarah was sitting beside someone else. When she saw Abraham, she smiled and shrugged.

He found an empty seat at the back and sat down. He watched the other kids talking and laughing. Nobody seemed to notice he was there. He looked out the window and imagined a knight on horseback running beside the bus, leaping over parked cars, weaving in and out of traffic, the knight's armour gleaming in the dull sunlight.

The bus pulled into the parking lot. Abraham was the last one off. He walked to class alone.

The door was closed when he got there. He turned the knob and opened the door. Mrs. Picadia didn't seem to notice. He snuck in and slid behind his desk. He took his books from his backpack, pretending he'd been there the whole time.

"Now class," Mrs. Picadia said, opening the textbook on her desk, "who can tell me what the largest ocean on the planet is?"

Abraham's hand shot up. A few other students slowly raised theirs.

"Yes, Mya?"

"The Pacific Ocean."

"Why, yes. That's correct. Now, do you know why it's called that?"

"I... uh... no."

"That's okay, Mya. It's a tough question. Maybe somebody else in the class knows?"

Abraham raised his hand.

"Vince. Go ahead."

"Because it's pacific?"

Mrs. P smiled. "Well, you're not wrong. But can you tell me what pacific means?"

"It means... uh... um."

"Anybody else? What does the word pacific mean?"

Abraham waited. No one else put up their hand. His crept towards the ceiling.

"Anyone?" Mrs. P asked, her eyes scanning the classroom.

Abraham reached higher. Didn't she see him? He waved his hand.

Mrs. P looked down at the textbook. "It means... peaceful or calm. Pacific means peaceful or calm."

His hand dropped like a deflating helium balloon.

*

The bell rang for recess. Abraham ran onto the field and joined the group of kids there.

"First captain, second pick," Vince said, one foot resting on the ball.

"Second captain, first pick," said a kid from a higher grade. "Ryan, you're with me."

Ryan's eyes widened and he pointed at himself. "Me?"

"If you don't hurry, I might change my mind."

The kids laughed.

Vince picked a girl. She flipped her long hair and ran over to stand beside him.

Abraham looked at his feet. Vince usually picked him first. What was the deal? Then again, Ryan had never been picked first. Maybe they were in on a prank.

The second captain picked again, then Vince. They kept going, their teams growing, till only Abraham and a boy with a cast on his arm were left. It was Vince's pick. Abraham stared at him.

"Jordan," Vince said. The kid looked at Abraham and shrugged.

Abraham ran over to the second captain's team. "You're in net," he said to Abraham.

Squatting at the top of the box, Abraham watched the action unfold at the other end of the field. His team was controlling the ball as it had for most of the game. Abraham had faced a few shots but they'd either gone wide or high. Still, his team only had one goal. Vince's goalkeeper, a red-haired kid, was standing on his head.

Abraham watched as Ryan took a shot, a weak punt that didn't leave the ground. The keeper knelt, swallowed it up and heaved it back out to the defender, the long-haired girl, who forwarded the ball to Vince just shy of centrefield.

Abraham stood, suddenly alert. His team fell back into defensive positions. Vince dribbled, cautiously advancing the ball. He crossed it to the right winger who carried it upfield. The girl surged up the left wing. A perfect pass from the winger and a lone defender separated her from Abraham. Vince charged. The girl cheated inside, and Abraham left her to the defender, scrambling towards the open lane. Sure enough, the ball was headed for Vince, who wound up and fired.

Abraham slid on his knees and turned, the ball hitting him in the stomach. He keeled over, holding onto it, unable to breathe. He gasped but his lungs wouldn't fill up.

Ryan ran over.

"He's fine," Vince said, backing away. "He's just winded."

"Lift your arms," Ryan said.

Abraham reached for the sky and his lungs inflated. He slowly stood up.

"Let's go," Vince said. "Clock's running down!"

"Are you okay?" Ryan asked.

"Yeah, I'm fine," Abraham said, shooting Vince a glare. He picked up the ball, set it on the corner and kicked.

*

On the bus ride home, Sarah was sitting beside some other kid. The only open seat was beside Ryan.

"Hey Abraham!" he said, scrunching his face to move his glasses up his nose. "Good job in net today."

"Thanks, Ryan. You had a really good chance near the end there."

"Thanks for saying so. You can't win 'em all, I guess. How's your stomach?"

"It's fine. Felt fine after a few seconds." Seeing Sarah talk to another boy made it burn again.

"Vince was kind of a jerk about it, huh?"

"He's just competitive, that's all."

"He sure is. Say, how come you aren't sitting with Sarah today?"

"I'm not sure. She was sitting with one of her friends this morning and with this kid now."

"You haven't talked to her?"

"I haven't had the chance."

"Well if you want me to give her a note or something for you, I can do that."

Abraham smiled. "Thanks, Ryan."

"No problem. That's what friends are for, right?"

*

Abraham dumped his backpack by the front door and ran into the kitchen.

Mom was sliding a casserole into the oven. "Oh hi, honey. How was school?"

On the counter was the torn doll.

She followed his gaze. "What is that thing?"

He shrugged. "I don't know. I found it on the sidewalk. Maybe somebody dropped it?"

She wiped her hands on her apron and picked up the top half. "Look at his little bowtie! Kind of looks like you, doesn't it?"

*

Abraham hadn't been in the treehouse since his birthday. A bird's nest sat in the corner surrounded by spatters of white.

"Abraham!" Dad yelled from the back door. "Dinner's almost ready!"

He crouched and held his breath.

"Quit playing around, I know you're in there." The screen door wheezed shut.

Abraham sighed.

*

Abraham woke to the ringing of his alarm clock. He groaned and rubbed his eyes. He fumbled for the clock, switched it off, rolled over and dozed again.

"Get up," Mom yelled through the door, "or you'll miss the bus!"

He looked at the clock and leapt out of bed.

He burst out the front door as the bus turned the corner, leaving behind a plume of blue smoke. He cinched the straps of his backpack and started to walk.

*

Abraham quietly closed the door to the classroom.

"Late again, Abraham?" Mrs. P said. The other kids tittered. He slunk to his desk and put his head down.

At recess he watched the kids run onto the field. He looked at his feet. He didn't feel like playing today. He spotted Sarah sitting at the top of the monkey bars talking to another girl. He thought about going over to say hi but didn't want to interrupt.

After class, Mrs. P had Abraham stay behind to clean the blackboard erasers. White chalk dust clouded around him as he banged the erasers together, coughing.

The bus was gone when he was finally done. He walked home, casting a glance at the brown, one-storey house as he passed.

*

After dinner he went to his room. He lay on the bed and stared at the ceiling. Something had changed. Ever since he told Mya he didn't want to play her game anymore, people were treating him differently. Worse. He rolled onto his side and stared at the wall.

Was she playing the game still? Was this all part of it?

No, it couldn't be. She said she never made anyone do anything — she just made it so Abraham got what he wanted. But how could she do that without making them do it?

He thought of Ryan on the bus, offering to give Sarah a note for him. Abraham hadn't even asked Ryan to do that; he just wanted to. But why? He'd told Ryan how he hadn't talked to Sarah... and he just offered. "What's what friends are for," he'd said.

He told Ryan about his problem... and because Ryan's his friend... he offered to help! Abraham sat upright. Was that it? Was it that simple? It couldn't be.

He looked around the room. He saw the toys he'd gotten for his birthday, some still in their packaging, piled in the corner; the photos Mom took of him and his friends on his birthday pinned to the corkboard; the certificate from the public speaking contest hanging in a frame over his desk; the corner of one of Sarah's notes sticking out of the top drawer of his dresser; and there on top, a dust outline of where the soccer trophy had been.

It was all real, and it was all his — whether it was thanks to Mya's game or not. He'd scored the goals, he'd recited the speech, he'd penned the love letters. He'd done it all on his own. Sure, he couldn't have scored the goals without his teammates (or Coach) or done the speech without Mrs. P (well, maybe he could have) — but they'd all done it together because they all wanted to win.

And the letters.... his heart panged. Well, he wouldn't have written one if Sarah hadn't first. He thought of her smiling and shrugging the other morning on the bus. Of her sitting with the other kid that same afternoon. Maybe she didn't like him anymore. What did that have to do with Mya's game? Maybe she did still like him.

He sighed and flopped back on the bed. There was only one way to know for sure. But it couldn't be that simple... could it?

Twelve

ABRAHAM PUT UP his hand.

Mrs. P looked right through him as she scanned the class.

"Ryan?"

"Abraham has his hand up."

"Thank you, Ryan, but I'm asking you."

He sunk into his chair. "I don't know."

Mrs. P sighed. "Does anybody know?"

Abraham's hand was still up. She looked down at the textbook and adjusted her glasses. She opened her mouth.

"Jupiter," Abraham muttered.

"The answer," Mrs. P said, "is ... Jupiter. Now. Who can tell me what the second-largest planet is?"

*

At recess, Abraham saw Mya standing by the tetherball pole.

"You want to play?" he asked.

"How come you aren't playing soccer with the other kids?"

"Last time I played I was picked last. I had to be the goalie. And Vince kicked the ball at my stomach so hard that I couldn't breathe."

She smiled. "I'm sorry."

"It's okay, that's part of the game."

"Were you scared when you couldn't breathe?"

"Yeah, but it went away soon enough. What hurt more was Vince not picking me and acting like we weren't friends anymore."

Mya looked away.

"I guess I know what it feels like now. I'm sorry, Mya. I'm sorry for saying I didn't want to play with you."

Her eyes were about to overflow.

"So... do you want to play tetherball?"

She shook her head and ran away.

*

After the bell rang, the class cleared out. Mrs. P was rearranging her desk when Abraham approached.

"Mrs. P?"

Her eyes widened. "Yes, Abraham."

"I... uh." He looked at his shoes. The clock ticked.

"What is it, Abraham?"

He swallowed. "I... I want to know why you never pick me when I put up my hand."

Mrs. P's mouth fell open. "Why... whatever do you mean, Abraham? I try to give all my students a fair chance to answer."

He twisted the toe of his sneaker on the floor. It squeaked. "Every time I put up my hand to answer a question, you ignore me."

"Every time, Abraham?"

"Well, it happened at least twice today. Even Ryan noticed and he sits in front of me."

Mrs. P slammed the cover of the textbook closed and pressed down. "Abraham, it's not easy for me to accept criticism. I have been teaching for a long time — longer than you've been alive — and my evaluations are always very, very positive."

"Sorry, Mrs. P." Wait a minute, he thought. Why was he sorry? He hadn't done anything wrong. She was the one ignoring him! And yes — lately, it had been every time! "You know what, Mrs. P?"

"What is it?"

"I think you're a very nice person, and I don't doubt that you're a good teacher. But you're an adult, and I'm just a kid. And you're supposed to be teaching me—"

"Supposed to be?"

"Hold on a minute, please. I don't mean to disrespect you" — his vision went blurry — "and this is very hard for me to say. But I think you should listen to me this time. Because I'm trying to help you get better at your job by telling you how you can help me." He dropped his head. A tear fell.

The clock ticked.

"Abraham, look at me. I can tell it was harder for you to say that than it was for me to hear it. And I know you wouldn't talk to me about it if it wasn't important to you. So thank you."

He looked up.

"And I'll take what you've said into consideration. As I said, I try to be fair with my students. Maybe" — she leaned forward — "I've just heard you give the right answer so many times that I know I don't need to worry about you knowing it."

He smiled. "Not like Ryan."

She laughed. "No, not like Ryan. Anyway, thank you for coming to talk to me. I'll do my best to be more fair when I'm asking the class for answers to my questions — even though I know you're a sharp cookie. Maybe, if nothing else, it will encourage the other students to try harder." She placed the textbook into her briefcase. "I'll see you tomorrow, Abraham."

He was already halfway to the door.

Outside, the bus loosed a cloud of black exhaust and lurched away from the sidewalk.

Not today, Abraham thought. He tightened the straps of his backpack and broke into a trot.

The bus slowed as it neared the end of the parking lot. He lowered his head and pumped his fists.

The bus straightened out from the turn and chugged, spewing another plume of smoke.

Not today!

It slowed as it neared a stop sign and he closed the gap. It rolled through the stop and he dug deep. Running just behind it, he reached out, stretching as far as he could — and slapped the side of the bus.

It kept going.

Not! Today!

The bus accelerated. Summoning all his strength, he matched its speed and stretched out again. He rapped the side of the bus with his knuckles. A window opened.

"Abraham!"

"Sarah!"

"Mr. H, stop!"

The brakes squealed.

Panting, Abraham approached the opening door.

"Sorry about that, little man," Mr. Hallick said. "I didn't see you there! Good hustle though, I gotta say."

"Thanks, Mr. H." He turned to look down the aisle. Sarah was smiling at him but the seat beside her was taken by that other kid. Behind her, Ryan waved. He waved back and started down the aisle.

"Hi, Abraham!"

"Wow you're fast!"

"Good job, Abraham!"

He got to Sarah's row. Ryan narrowed his eyes; Abraham nodded. Ryan smiled.

"Excuse me," Abraham said to the boy sitting beside Sarah, "do you mind if I sit there today?"

The boy looked at Sarah, who was smiling at Abraham, and back at him. "I guess," he mumbled, shuffling out of the seat.

Abraham and Sarah exchanged a glance and sat quiet for a moment.

"Thanks for asking Mr. H to stop," he said at last.

She pushed a strand of hair behind her ear. "You're welcome. You looked like you could've run all the way home, but I figured I would save you the effort."

They laughed.

He looked at her and swallowed. "Say, Sarah—"

"I'm sorry for ignoring you lately. I—"

"No, no. It's okay. You don't have to say sorry. I'm the one who should apologize."

"Yeah? How come?"

"Well... when I saw you sitting with other kids, I thought it meant..." — he looked at her smiling, freckled face, her wavy auburn hair — "I thought it meant that you didn't like me anymore."

"No, Abraham! That's—"

"Hold on a sec. And instead of talking to you to ask what the matter was, I assumed the worst and just started to feel sorry for myself."

"It's not that at all! I thought you didn't like me anymore! When you didn't get on the bus, I felt silly saving you a seat just to sit by myself. So when" — she nodded backwards — "asked to sit, I couldn't think of a reason to say no."

His heart leapt.

"So I was happy to see you running after the bus today" — she leaned in and whispered — "and very happy you asked him to move. He smells like cheese."

Something touched Abraham's hand: Sarah's. Their fingers intertwined.

"You think I'd forget about my knight in shining armour?" She lay her head on his shoulder. "You saved my life."

"Well, your leg at least."

They laughed.

Thirteen

SIR CALIDAS DISMOUNTED his formidable steed Cygnus and threw away the splintered lance. The malevolent druid Okenower lay gasping, trapped under the weight of the disembowelled wolf he'd been riding.

He fixed Calidas with his beady black eyes. "Well Calidas," he rasped, "will you show me mercy and finish me off as you did my brother?"

Calidas knelt and put his shoulder against the dead beast's spine. He planted his boots and with a great shove moved the carcass from atop the wizard.

Okenower cackled. "Mercy, indeed!" He sprang to his feet. "Would you have me believe that you will allow me to walk away from this battle with my life?"

"What you choose to believe is up to you." Calidas rose. "But I see no need for this mortal antagonism to continue. The princess is free; my task is accomplished."

The wizard's eyes narrowed. "What trickery is this, knight?"

"None at all. Though you bear me a grudge for the death of your brother, I wonder if you might reconsider it for sparing your life."

Okenower stood motionless. The dawn sun broke over the horizon.

"As sure as the sun rises every day to dispel the darkness, I hereby vouchsafe your life with mine. Should you betray that oath, however, I will not hesitate to hunt you down again and run you through where you stand."

The wizard bared the gaps between his teeth. "An unexpected turn of events, knight, but not an unwanted one." He withdrew a hand into its sleeve. It emerged clutching a glowing green stone. "Should you ever require the skills of a magician" — he tossed the jewel — "peer into this stone and know that I will do whatever is in my power to aid you."

Calidas caught the stone. He looked upon it and tucked it into a pouch around his neck. "I am indebted to you, druid."

"No, knight. It is I who am indebted to you." He drew his cloak over his face and disappeared like a shadow into darkness.

Cygnus whinnied. Calidas laughed and caressed his muzzle. "Yes, yes. I haven't forgotten. All the oats you could possibly eat await at the royal stables. And if you hie us there with enough speed—"

"Abraham!" It was Mom. "Bed time!"

He looked at the mounted toy knight in his hand and the plastic wolf lying on the carpet. He scooped them into a box and tucked it away in the cupboard. He turned off the light and went upstairs.

*

Sitting beside Sarah on the bus, Abraham saw Mya walking to school by herself. He waved and thought she saw but she didn't wave back.

At recess Abraham chased the other kids onto the field. He stood at the back.

Vince lifted his ball in the air. "First captain, second pick."

"Second captain, first pick," said the red-headed boy. "Eeny, meeny, money, mo." He pointed at a different kid with each word.

No way Vince will see me back here, Abraham thought. He tapped the shoulder of the kid in front of him.

"Huh?"

"Sorry, I need to get to the front." He squeezed by.

"My mother told me..."

He snaked around the next kid.

"To pick the very best one..."

One kid stood between Abraham and the front of the crowd. He tapped his shoulder but the kid just shrugged. "Excuse me," he said, but the kid wouldn't move.

"And you are it!"

"Me?" the kid said.

"Yeah, you!"

The kid joined his captain. Abraham was at the front!

Vince slapped the ball and scanned the crowd. Abraham raised his hand but Vince looked right past him. He raised his other hand and Vince still ignored him. He jumped up and down, waving his arms. A few of the kids laughed but Vince still didn't look.

Abraham took a step forward, turned a cartwheel and stuck the landing. The kids clapped and cheered.

Vince smiled. "Get over here, you goof!"

Abraham bowed and stood beside his captain.

Once the teams were picked, the players took the field. Abraham volunteered for defence and positioned himself on the left side. Vince drew the ball back and offloaded it to Abraham.

Before long, the score was tied at one each. The opposing team came on strong. Abraham back-pedalled; Vince was caught deep in the offensive end. The winger — the kid who wouldn't get out of Abraham's way — closed the gap. He charged with a long dribble. Abraham tried to intercept but the kid was too fast. They collided; Abraham fell to the ground. The winger pressed on. The keeper came out to challenge. The ball left the winger's foot and hit the back of the net.

Abraham punched the ground. The winger, running back to high-five his teammates, stuck his tongue out at him.

Vince ran over and held out a hand. "That kid's tougher than he looks."

"Thanks. And faster. I thought I could beat him to the ball."

Play resumed. Vince tapped the ball to the right winger who advanced a few paces, turned and booted it back to Abraham's partner. He advanced to the centreline. The opponents fell back, leaving an ample cushion. The defenceman lobbed the ball across and deep. Vince was there to catch it on his chest and skip it back to Abraham.

He didn't have much room to play with, or time. All eyes were on him as he considered his options. The keeper was at the edge of the box; the defenders were sticking to them like glue. Vince and the tough kid jostled, and Vince gained some space. Abraham struck, aiming for Vince's side of the net but low. As if he'd read Abraham's mind, Vince sprinted towards the net as the keeper peeled back — but too late. Vince hopped and redirected the shot with his foot to tuck it inside the post.

Abraham and Vince ran towards each other.

"What a goal!"

"What a pass!"

The tough kid kicked the air and his shoe flew off. He chased it, hopping on one foot.

The bell rang and the kids headed back to their classrooms.

"Glad you picked me?" Abraham asked.

"Are you kidding? That was great! I just wish you still played for the Wolves."

"Wait... what do you mean?"

"Coach said that you'd quit. I thought you thought you were too good for us or something."

Coach said he'd quit? Was it because of what happened with him and Mya? "Is that why you... you didn't pick me the other day?"

"Yeah, why would I want to play with someone who doesn't want to play with me?"

"Fair enough."

"Anyway, I hope you and Coach can figure something out, because he's got Kareem playing your position, and well..."

"Enough said!"

*

When Abraham got home, he went to his room before going to the kitchen.

"Mom?"

She was stirring a pot on the stove. "Yes, honey."

"Can you help me with something?"

"Of course!" She put the spoon down and turned around. "What is it?"

He held up the two torn pieces of Mya's doll.

She crossed her arms. "Is there something you should be telling me?"

*

Abraham ran out the front door holding a box in his hands. He slowed when he got to the brown, one-story house and walked up to the door. He took a deep breath and knocked. It opened.

"Well well well," Coach said. "Look who it is. The boy who made my girl cry."

"Hi Coach." He clutched the box. "Is Mya home? I'd like to give her something to say sorry."

"There's only one thing you can do to make her happy again. Otherwise you're only gonna make it worse." He crossed his arms. "You sure you want to see her?"

"Yes, Coach."

Coach turned towards the hallway. "Mya! Someone's here to see you." He shot Abraham a glare. He went into the living room and sat in an armchair in front of the TV.

Mya poked her head around the corner. "What do you want?"

"I came to say sorry."

"You already said sorry."

"I came to say sorry" — he held out the box — "and show you I mean it."

She crept around the corner and reached for the box. Abraham handed it over. Coach watched from the living room, mouth hanging open.

"What is it?" Mya asked.

"Open it."

She lifted the lid and her eyes lit up. She dropped the lid and grabbed the doll. It was sewn together with purple thread that looked like a belt. She let the box fall and hugged the doll against her chest. Coach smiled and turned back to the TV.

“Does this mean… you want to play again?”

Abraham laughed. “Yes, but why don’t we play a different game this time?”

!

"NEXT UP, FROM RIVERTIDE ELEMENTARY, is Abraham and his speech on India." The master of ceremonies looked back and clapped.

Abraham stuck his finger between his shirt collar and neck and tugged. The high school gym was a lot bigger than his school's — and since it was the district final, there were a lot more people in it.

He stood and walked towards the microphone in the centre of the spotlight. It was hot on his head. He coughed and the speakers squealed. He tugged at his shirt collar again.

Mom and Dad waved from the middle of the crowd. To their right and up a few rows, Mrs. Picadia peered out from her cat-eye glasses. He remembered what she'd said. He took a deep breath, imagining air coming through the soles of his feet.

He opened his mouth — and closed it again. He looked down at his shoes. Up at Mom and Dad, who smiled. At

Mrs. P, who nodded. Towards the judges, who were staring at him. Somebody in the audience coughed.

Abraham raised his hand, palm up, towards the judges. “Esteemed judges...”

*

When Abraham came out from backstage, Mom and Dad were standing with Mrs. P.

“There he is!” Dad said. Mrs. P clapped.

Mom knelt and Abraham ran into her arms. “I’m so proud of you, honey!”

“Me too,” Dad said, tousling his hair.

“We all are,” Mrs. P said.

Mom stood up. “So... let’s see it!”

Abraham reached under the neck of his sweater and pulled out the medal.

“Ooh!”

“Aah!”

“I hope you’ll bring that to show the class!”

Abraham looked at the prize, his eyes shining.

Made in the USA
Monee, IL
31 May 2021

69869526R00059